Shirley Barber's

FAIRY STORIES
BUMPER COLLECTION

Table of Contents

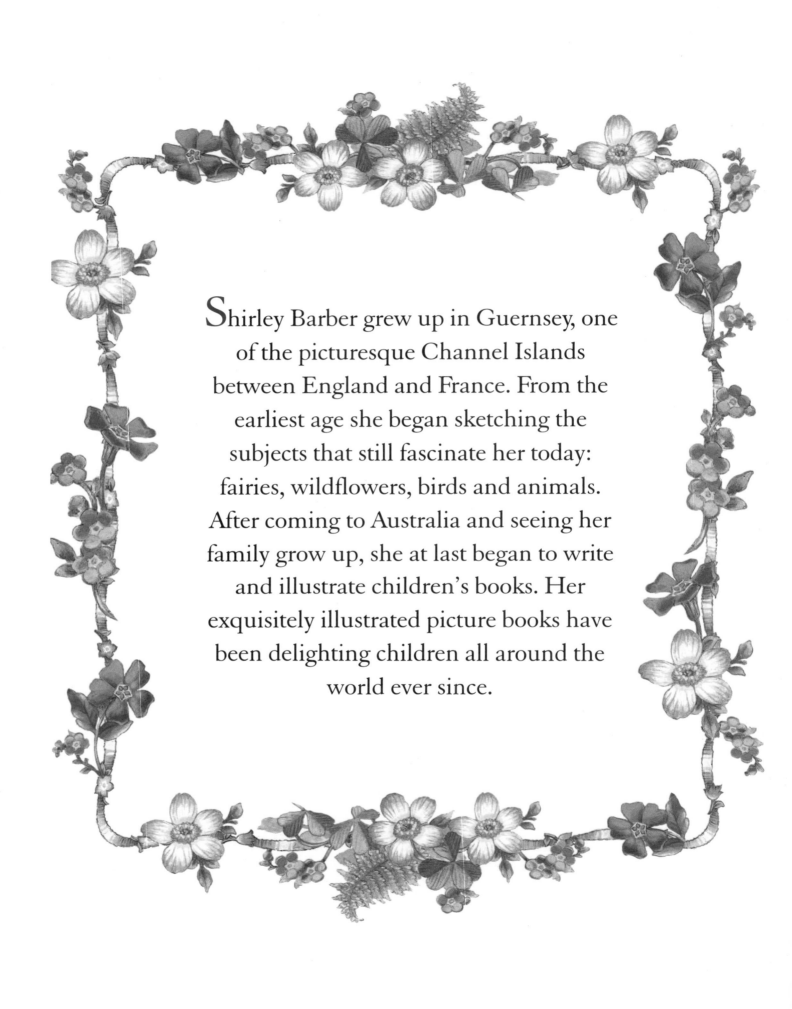

Shirley Barber grew up in Guernsey, one of the picturesque Channel Islands between England and France. From the earliest age she began sketching the subjects that still fascinate her today: fairies, wildflowers, birds and animals. After coming to Australia and seeing her family grow up, she at last began to write and illustrate children's books. Her exquisitely illustrated picture books have been delighting children all around the world ever since.

BEDTIME STORIES

The Royal Jewellers

$\mathscr{U}$nder the hedge by a big green field stood a tiny shop called: 'Edwin Beetle & Son, Jewellers.' If you knelt down and peered through the window you could see Mr Beetle and his son Benny working in the shop while Mrs Beetle cooked the meals and looked after weeny Baby Beetle, asleep in his nutshell cradle.

The Beetles lived very comfortably until one day a huge red tractor started to plough up the green field beside their shop. The Beetles, terrified, packed up the few things they could carry and fled till they reached the forests of Fairyland.

"If we aren't safe living in Fairyland," said Mrs Beetle firmly, "well, I don't know where we can go, indeed I don't!" So, among the twisted roots of a large tree, they set up their tiny new shop with their home behind it.

3

At first, very few customers stopped to look at the necklaces and rings. Mr Beetle would sadly shake his head, remembering the nice shop and home he had once had. Nothing would ever be the same again, he thought.

Then, one day, a beautiful golden fairy stopped and looked at the tiny shop in surprise. She knelt down so she could see better, and Mr Beetle and Benny proudly showed her their finest jewellery.

"These are wonderfully made," said the golden fairy. "Your work is so fine. May I take three necklaces to show the Fairy Queen?"

Mr Beetle made haste to wrap the necklaces in flower petals, tying them into neat parcels with grass blades, and gave them to the fairy. The next day the golden fairy reappeared.

"Mr Beetle, the Queen loves your necklaces and she wants to buy all three," she said smiling. "She offers you three wishes in payment, and she would also like to order a very special tiara, with a matching necklace and bracelet, to be made in gold and many coloured precious gems."

Mr Beetle was at first delighted, but then he became anxious. Where could he get all the gold and different

coloured jewels he would need for such an order? "Dearie me!" chuckled Mrs Beetle. "You've got three wishes, haven't you? Wish first for a gold and jewel mine deep beneath this tree, second for a lovely new shop that's big enough to live in too, and third for a food cupboard that fills up again after you've taken things out!"

So that is what he did. Now, a quaint little shop stands among the twisted tree roots. Inside, Mr Beetle is always busy at his workbench, while Mrs Beetle looks after Baby Beetle, and cooks such delicious treats that there is nearly always a visitor dropping in for a chat and a slice of freshly baked cake. And every time Mr Beetle needs another diamond or an emerald or a gold nugget, Benny nips down the tunnel to the mine below.

Whenever anyone is sad about their life, Mrs Beetle simply smiles and says, "Never give up hope! Look at us! We lost everything, then overnight things changed and here we are better off than we ever were before!"

The Unicorns

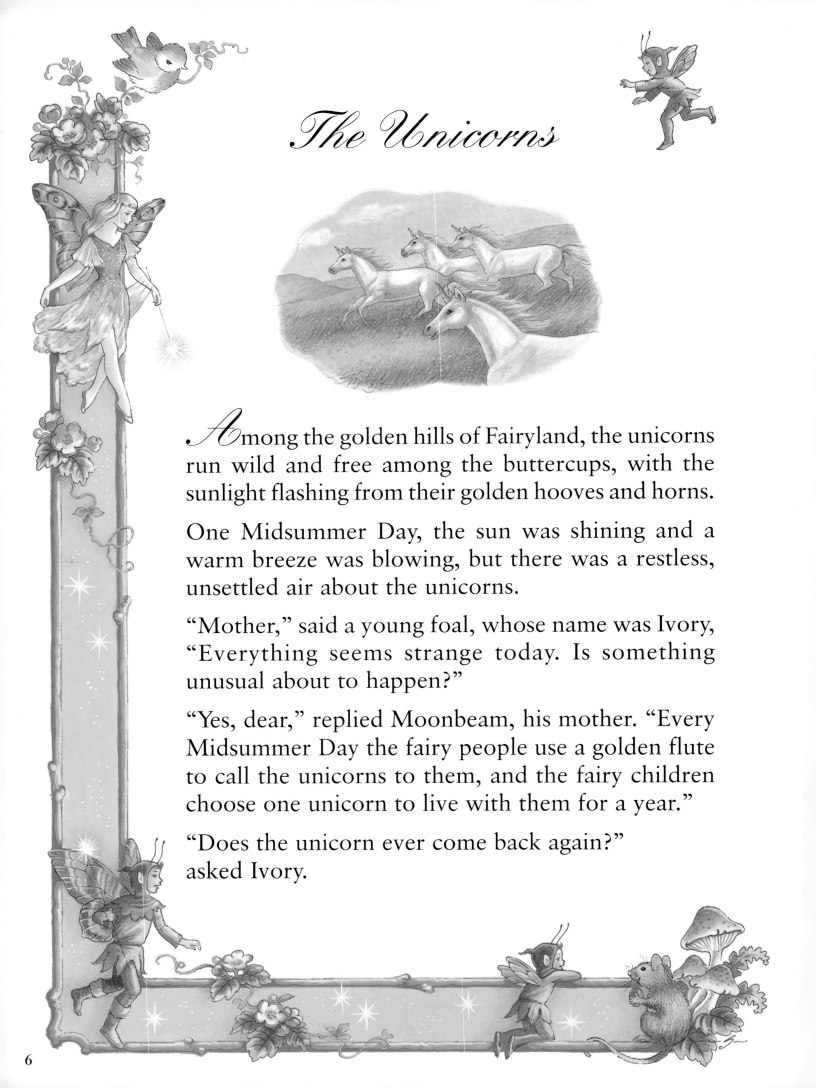

Among the golden hills of Fairyland, the unicorns run wild and free among the buttercups, with the sunlight flashing from their golden hooves and horns.

One Midsummer Day, the sun was shining and a warm breeze was blowing, but there was a restless, unsettled air about the unicorns.

"Mother," said a young foal, whose name was Ivory, "Everything seems strange today. Is something unusual about to happen?"

"Yes, dear," replied Moonbeam, his mother. "Every Midsummer Day the fairy people use a golden flute to call the unicorns to them, and the fairy children choose one unicorn to live with them for a year."

"Does the unicorn ever come back again?" asked Ivory.

"Oh, yes," his mother replied. "When the fairies choose a new unicorn, they return the one who was chosen the year before. Each unicorn spends a year at the Fairy Palace learning how to be gentle and obedient for the fairy children."

"If they choose me," said Ivory, "I shall say, 'No, I don't want to go.' I want to stay with you, Mother, always."

Moonbeam lifted her head and lovingly nuzzled her young foal. "Dear one, if you are called by the golden flute you can't help but go. It plays a magical note that unicorns can't resist."

Ivory tossed his head and went for a canter, his white mane and tail streaming in the fresh breeze. He was half a hillside away when a distant sweet fluting brought him to a surprised halt. He found he could not help but turn towards it, and soon, quite against his will, he was cantering back to all the other unicorns on the hillside.

There he saw the fairy folk and the flute player for the first time. They were laughing and singing as they made their way along the lane which led up from the lower regions of Fairyland. The fairy children saw Ivory and called joyfully, "That one! Oh, let's choose that one!"

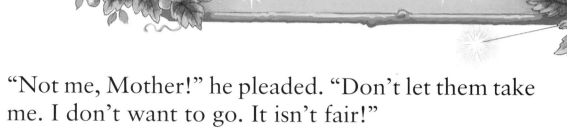

"Not me, Mother!" he pleaded. "Don't let them take me. I don't want to go. It isn't fair!"

Moonbeam gave him a velvet kiss. "Little son, it is an honour to be chosen by the fairies and you must go. We'll soon be together again." Then the fairies placed a garland of flowers around Ivory's neck, and he went with them to Fairyland.

A year passed and once again it was Midsummer Day. Moonbeam stood patiently with the rest of the unicorns as the fairies chose a new unicorn to take to Fairyland. Ivory was released by the fairy children and trotted briskly up to her.

They nuzzled lovingly. Moonbeam said, "You've grown, little son. And was it so bad after all?"

Ivory looked embarrassed. "I missed you, Mother, but I had a really good time, and they told me I was the nicest pet unicorn they ever had."

Then he kicked up his golden heels and galloped away, scattering butterflies and flower petals, and enjoying his freedom once again.

Wilfrid's New Friend

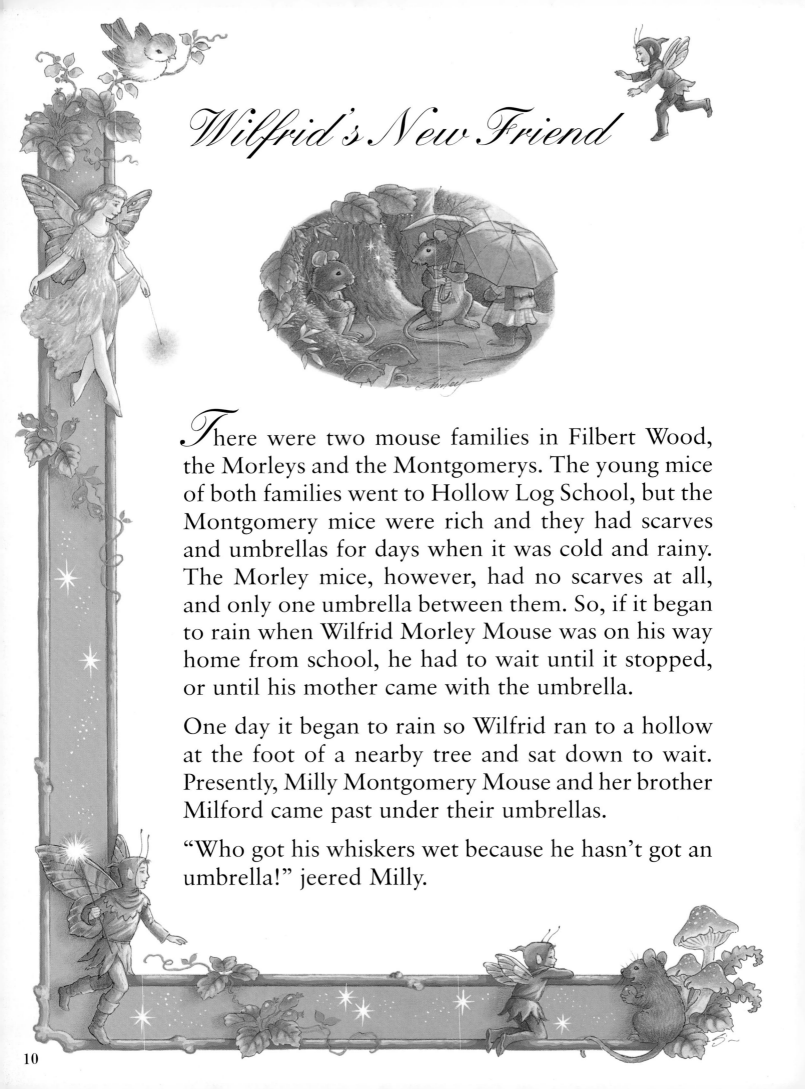

There were two mouse families in Filbert Wood, the Morleys and the Montgomerys. The young mice of both families went to Hollow Log School, but the Montgomery mice were rich and they had scarves and umbrellas for days when it was cold and rainy. The Morley mice, however, had no scarves at all, and only one umbrella between them. So, if it began to rain when Wilfrid Morley Mouse was on his way home from school, he had to wait until it stopped, or until his mother came with the umbrella.

One day it began to rain so Wilfrid ran to a hollow at the foot of a nearby tree and sat down to wait. Presently, Milly Montgomery Mouse and her brother Milford came past under their umbrellas.

"Who got his whiskers wet because he hasn't got an umbrella!" jeered Milly.

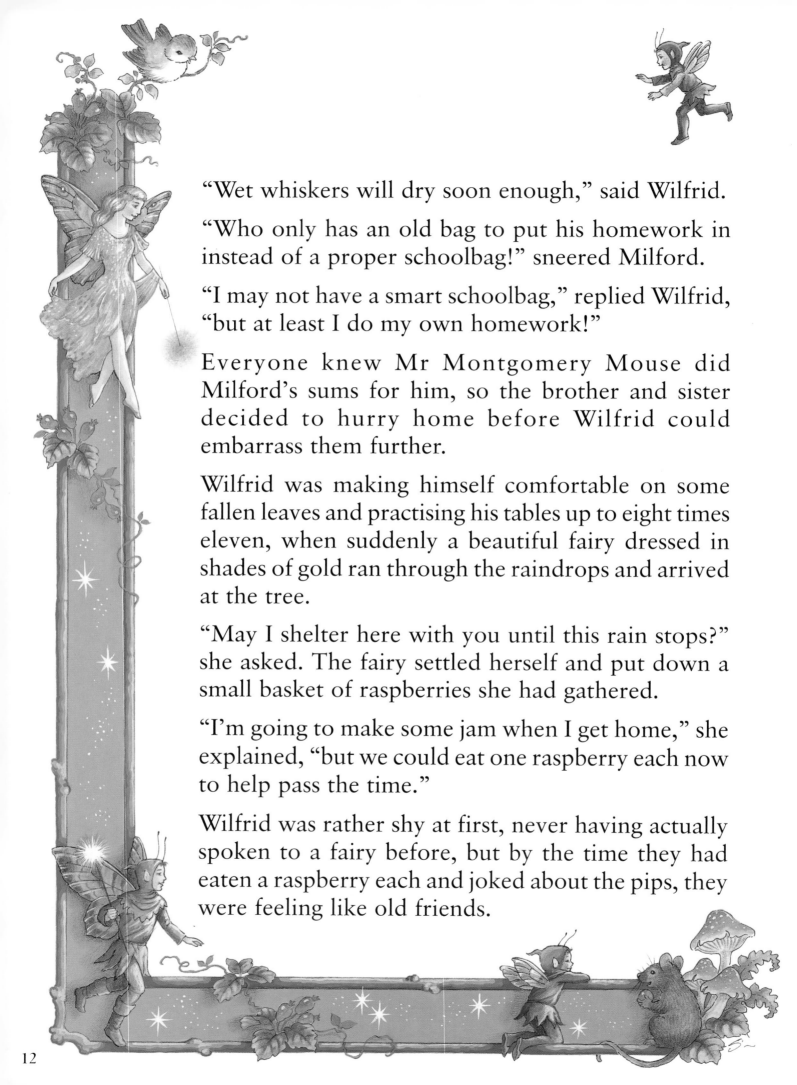

"Wet whiskers will dry soon enough," said Wilfrid.

"Who only has an old bag to put his homework in instead of a proper schoolbag!" sneered Milford.

"I may not have a smart schoolbag," replied Wilfrid, "but at least I do my own homework!"

Everyone knew Mr Montgomery Mouse did Milford's sums for him, so the brother and sister decided to hurry home before Wilfrid could embarrass them further.

Wilfrid was making himself comfortable on some fallen leaves and practising his tables up to eight times eleven, when suddenly a beautiful fairy dressed in shades of gold ran through the raindrops and arrived at the tree.

"May I shelter here with you until this rain stops?" she asked. The fairy settled herself and put down a small basket of raspberries she had gathered.

"I'm going to make some jam when I get home," she explained, "but we could eat one raspberry each now to help pass the time."

Wilfrid was rather shy at first, never having actually spoken to a fairy before, but by the time they had eaten a raspberry each and joked about the pips, they were feeling like old friends.

Then they played 'I-spy-with-my-little-eye', and later Wilfrid showed the fairy how to play noughts and crosses using the back page of his schoolbook. As they played the rain slowed, and soon Mrs Morley Mouse appeared before them, under her big patched umbrella.

"There now, Wilfy," she chuckled. "Perhaps I needn't have come to meet you after all – the rain has almost stopped." Wilfrid introduced his new friend to his mother, and they talked for a little while until the sun was shining brightly again. Then the fairy said a smiling good-bye to the mice and promised to call by in a few days with a pot of her raspberry jam.

"Well, you are a lucky mouse!" said Wilfrid's mother, "There's not many who get the chance to make friends with a real fairy."

"Yes," agreed Wilfrid, happily. "And do you know what, Mum? If we were rich and I had an umbrella of my own, I would never have met her at all!"

The Fairy Queen's Ruby Pendant

Elissa was Queen Elvira's younger sister. She was a beautiful, impulsive, kindhearted fairy, much loved by the pixies and all the fairy children.

The Queen would often say, "Elissa, you must quieten down. You are a fairy princess, so behave with dignity." Elissa would try to be good for a while, but before she knew it she would be running up the palace staircase again, while the fairy children chased after her with squeals of laughter.

Because of her high spirits, Elissa was often in trouble, and one day something really dreadful happened. The Queen was standing before her mirror admiring her ruby pendant. The ruby was a rare gem with a star glowing in its heart, given to her by the King to wear to the fairy ball.

Suddenly, Elissa burst into the room. She bumped into the Queen and knocked the pendant to the floor, where it broke into two pieces. "Elissa!" cried the Queen. "How could you be so clumsy! The ruby is ruined!"

The Queen was very upset. Elissa crept around like a mouse and wept. She knew she would not be allowed to go to the ball.

The day of the ball dawned and the fairy children came running to find their favourite playmate. "Come to the seashore with us, Elissa," they cried. "The tide is very low today, and we can see jewels in the rock pools just waiting for us to pick them up."

Elissa still felt sad but she was too kindhearted to refuse the children, so together they set off for the seashore. In spite of her sadness, she joined in the search and before long she spotted a magnificent gem. "Oh, look!" she cried. It was a ruby with a double star in its heart, the rarest of all gems to be found in Fairyland! Elissa hurried back to the palace and asked to see the King.

"Your Majesty," said Elissa respectfully, "I have found this beautiful gem and hope you will take it to give to my sister in place of the pendant I broke."

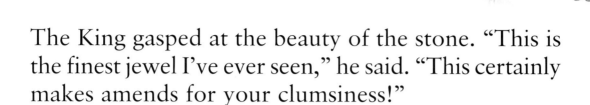

The King gasped at the beauty of the stone. "This is the finest jewel I've ever seen," he said. "This certainly makes amends for your clumsiness!"

Soon a new glittering double-starred pendant was presented to the Queen. The King explained where the beautiful jewel came from.

"Oh, Elissa," cried the Queen. "It is the most beautiful ruby. All is forgiven and forgotten – and of course you must come to the ball tonight!"

"Hooray!" shouted Elissa. She rushed out of the room, pursued by the fairy children, and the sound of her feet flying up the palace stairway could plainly be heard. The King and Queen looked at each other and smiled. Elissa hadn't changed – but perhaps they didn't really want her to!

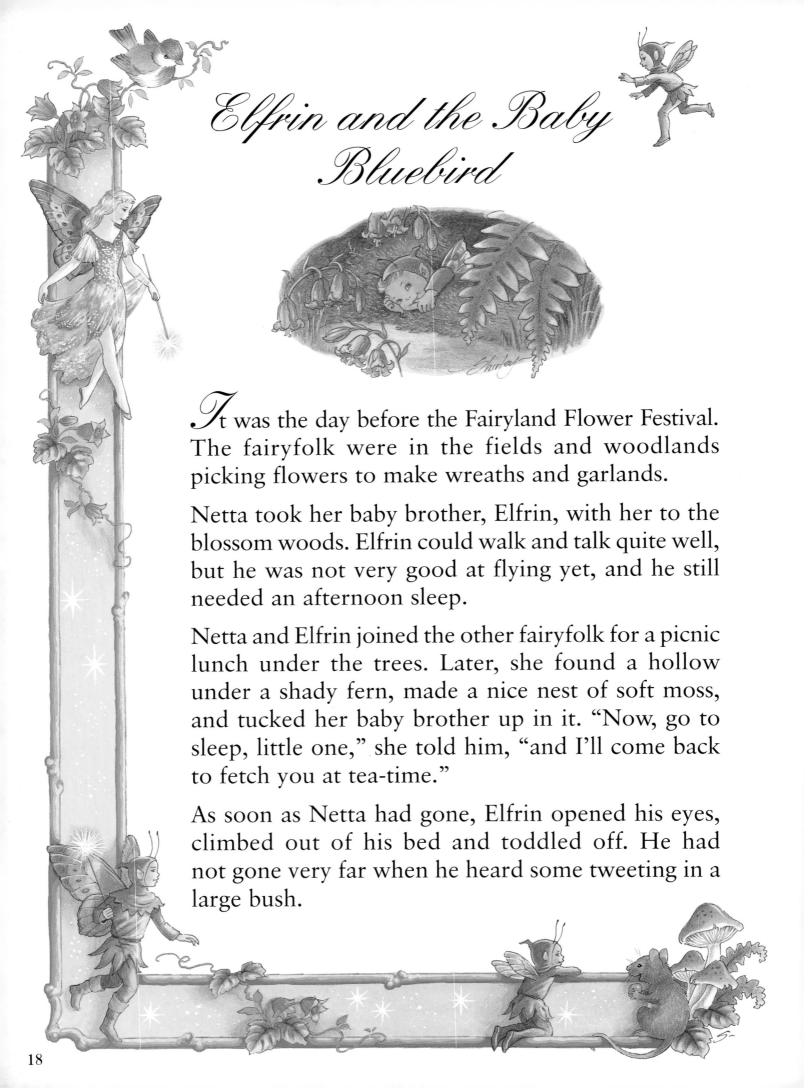

Elfrin and the Baby Bluebird

It was the day before the Fairyland Flower Festival. The fairyfolk were in the fields and woodlands picking flowers to make wreaths and garlands.

Netta took her baby brother, Elfrin, with her to the blossom woods. Elfrin could walk and talk quite well, but he was not very good at flying yet, and he still needed an afternoon sleep.

Netta and Elfrin joined the other fairyfolk for a picnic lunch under the trees. Later, she found a hollow under a shady fern, made a nice nest of soft moss, and tucked her baby brother up in it. "Now, go to sleep, little one," she told him, "and I'll come back to fetch you at tea-time."

As soon as Netta had gone, Elfrin opened his eyes, climbed out of his bed and toddled off. He had not gone very far when he heard some tweeting in a large bush.

He looked up and saw a baby bluebird flapping wildly on the edge of a nest. Suddenly it fell and landed on the soft moss in front of Elfrin.

"You naughty birdie," scolded Elfrin, "You should be sleeping in bed." He picked up the baby bird, puffing and panting, and lugged it back to his own nest under the fern.

"Now, go to sleep, little one," he said firmly, just like Netta, and off he toddled again.

Meanwhile, Mr. and Mrs. Bluebird fluttered back to their nest – and found the baby had gone! They flew into a panic, tweeting loudly, terrified that harm had come to their baby. They flew through the trees until they came to the nearest of the fairies – which happened to be Netta.

"Calm down," she told them. "Your baby can't be very far. I'll help you look for it."

Meanwhile, Elfrin had arrived back at the bluebirds' nest. He wondered if there were any more baby birds in it, so he climbed all the way up and out along a branch until he reached the nest. It was empty, but it was so cosy that Elfrin thought he would try it out. He climbed in and quickly fell asleep.

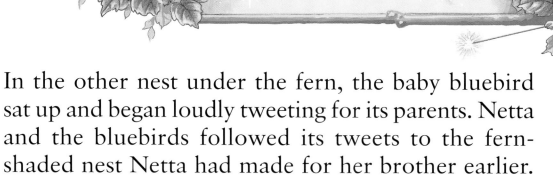

In the other nest under the fern, the baby bluebird sat up and began loudly tweeting for its parents. Netta and the bluebirds followed its tweets to the fern-shaded nest Netta had made for her brother earlier.

"Well, here is your baby – but where is my baby brother?" cried Netta, now rather worried herself.

"I wonder if….?" she murmured, then she flew off to the bush where the bluebirds had their nest. There she found her little brother fast asleep.

"What have you been up to, Elfrin?" laughed Netta. Elfrin opened his big blue eyes and yawned. "Tea-time?" he asked his sister.

"Yes, tea-time," smiled Netta. "And the bluebirds want their nest back, so unless you want earthworms for tea like a baby bluebird, you had better come home with me!"

Lost in the Forest

"*N*ow, children," said Mrs Rabbit one sunny afternoon, "I want you to go to Granny's burrow and give her a bottle of my violet cough syrup. When you arrive at the crossroads, take the path marked 'Primrose Lane', and that will lead you to Granny's home. But if you see those two Ratling brothers, don't stop to play with them because you know they're always getting into mischief!"

Off went Bobtail and Fluffkin, but when they reached the crossroads who should they see but the two naughty young rats leaning against the signpost. Bobtail hurried his sister Fluffkin along the path marked 'Primrose Lane', and away from the Ratlings who jeered and whistled rudely after them.

They soon reached Granny's burrow and she welcomed them with kisses and afternoon tea.

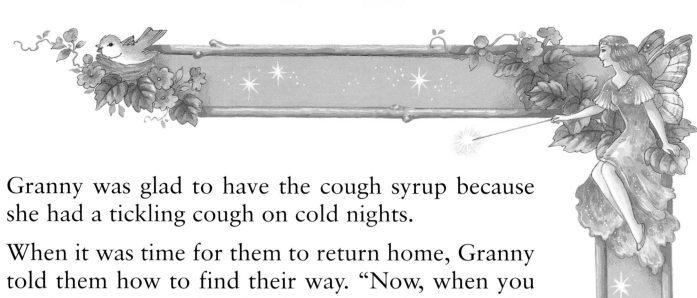

Granny was glad to have the cough syrup because she had a tickling cough on cold nights.

When it was time for them to return home, Granny told them how to find their way. "Now, when you reach the crossroads, take the path marked 'Cowslip Warren'," she said, "and then you will soon be safely home."

When Bobtail and Fluffkin arrived at the crossroads, they were glad to see the two rats had gone. "This sign says 'Cowslip Warren'," Bobtail told his sister, "and so that is our way home."

But soon they became worried. The path they were following seemed to be leading them deeper into the forest instead of home. Bobtail stopped. "Fluffkin, this must be the wrong path," he said. "I think we're lost. We must find a hole to spend the night, and tomorrow, when it's light, we'll try to find our way home."

But Bobtail couldn't find a hole deep enough to hide in, and he could hear a fox barking in the distance. Fluffkin was so frightened that she trembled.

Suddenly a beautiful blue fairy appeared before them holding a sparkling wand in her hand.

"Don't be afraid," she said. "I will use my magic to send the fox away on a long hunt, and I will teach those naughty Ratling brothers a lesson.

"They turned the signpost round so you would take the wrong path. That's why you became lost."

"And as for you, little bunnies, I will light my bluebell lamps and show you the way home!"

"Oh, thank you, kind fairy," chorused the little rabbits. Off they ran along the path towards home. The fairy's bluebell lamps lit up just ahead of them all the way, until they ran into the arms of their mother and father who were waiting for them at their own front door. After such an adventure in the dark forest they were safely home once more!

The ENCHANTED WOODS

Once upon a time, a little girl called Sarah Jane lived in a pretty cottage at the edge of a wood. The trees in the wood grew close together and on hot days she liked to sit in the shade and play with her toys.

There were ferns and flowers growing thickly between the trees and patches of wild strawberry plants. One warm sunny day, Sarah Jane wandered into the woods to play with her toys and look for wild strawberries.

Leaving her toys beneath a tree, she wandered further into the forest and found a few strawberries to put in her basket. All the while she had the strangest feeling she was being watched.

Eventually, she came to a big old tree and under the tree was a ring of mushrooms.

It was a magic fairy ring. But Sarah Jane didn't see it until after she had stepped inside. She stared at it, puzzled, and wondered what it was.

Suddenly Sarah Jane glimpsed a procession of fairies winding through the trees. Some were quaint and impish and others were the most beautiful creatures she had ever seen.

"Sarah Jane," they cried, "you are needed in Fairyland. Now that we've caught you in our magic fairy ring we can take you with us."

Then they waved their magic wands, and Sarah Jane felt herself become smaller and smaller.

She was now no taller than the fairies, and felt as light as thistledown. The fairies took her gently by the hands, and together they flew up above the treetops and out over a shimmering sea.

They landed on the shores of a strange and beautiful land. The flowers were taller than they were, and huge butterflies waited to greet them.

Soon, a messenger arrived from the fairy palace.

"Sarah Jane," he announced, "the Fairy King and Queen have been told of your arrival, and they would like to see you now."

So the fairies
sat Sarah Jane
on the back of
a butterfly,
and together
they flew
over a lake to
the fairy
palace, whose
golden turrets
sparkled in
the morning
sunlight.

The King and Queen welcomed Sarah Jane, and told her why she was needed in Fairyland.

"Our daughter is to be married to a prince from a neighbouring kingdom," said the Queen. "We need the presence of a mortal to ensure their good fortune and a happy marriage."

"Yes," said the King. "You will bring them good luck. Come, you will be our honoured guest and join us in our celebration."

Soon, it was time for the wedding. The chatter and laughter of the guests grew quiet as they gathered to watch the Prince and Princess exchange wedding vows.

After the wedding, a magnificent banquet was held in a glittering hall overlooking the lake. Sweet music was played by a band of funny little musicians while everyone, including Sarah Jane, feasted on the finest delicacies Fairyland could offer.

When the banquet was over, it was time for the Prince and Princess to leave. Together, they descended the golden stairway, as their guests cheered and showered them with rose petals. Then they climbed into a golden carriage drawn by dragonflies and flew off to their new home over the hills.

Now it was time for Sarah Jane to return home, too. The fairies flew with her over the sea and back to the fairy ring in the woods. They waved their magic wands, and once again she became her normal size.

"Goodbye, Sarah Jane," they said, dropping feather-light kisses upon her cheek. "You will always be our special friend."

Then she found herself alone in the woods once more with her basket and her toys beneath the shady tree.

Sarah Jane looked at her basket in amazement. It was overflowing with small, delicious strawberries. She picked up the basket and her toys and wandered home. Her family found it hard to believe her wonderful tale of how she had been a guest at a fairy wedding. But certainly, no one had ever seen so many wild strawberries as she had in her basket. They agreed that it must be a gift to her from the fairies, a sign to show she really *had* been to Fairyland.

RAINBOW MAGIC

Once upon a time,
there was an old lady called Gran Tibbett.
She lived in a farmhouse on the edge of the
forest with her granddaughter Annie and Little
Dog Bozo. Around the house was a pretty rose
garden, and around the garden was a grassy
meadow that went right to the edge
of the dark Fern Forest.

Early in the morning
the deer and their fawns would come out
of the forest and eat the grass in the meadow.
Sometimes Annie could get quite close to a fawn,
but Little Dog Bozo would run out and
bark at the big deer.
"One day they won't run away,"
Annie scolded. "Then you'll be sorry."
But Little Dog Bozo only laughed.

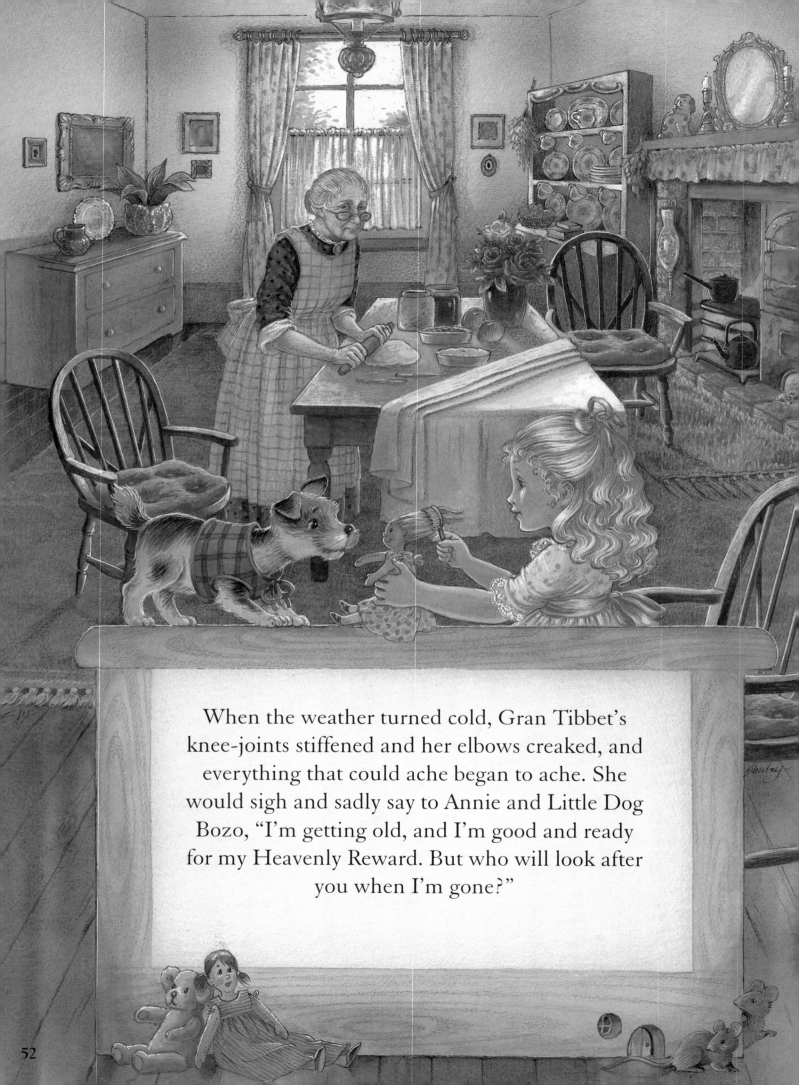

When the weather turned cold, Gran Tibbet's knee-joints stiffened and her elbows creaked, and everything that could ache began to ache. She would sigh and sadly say to Annie and Little Dog Bozo, "I'm getting old, and I'm good and ready for my Heavenly Reward. But who will look after you when I'm gone?"

But Annie and Little Dog Bozo were
not really worried because they felt sure Gran
would go on being Gran forever. They built
houses of dried fern fronds and made leaf boats,
and sailed them on the still water. A big fish lived
in the pool and if they kept very still, he rose to
look at them. But Bozo always barked and with a
splash the fish would be gone again.

On showery days, Annie sometimes saw a
rainbow so close she called to Gran, "Shall I run
to see if I can find the fairies' pot of gold at the
end of the rainbow?" But Gran said, "You keep
away from rainbows, Annie, They are very funny
things. You can get caught under rainbows, and
never come home again."

One day, when Annie and Little Dog Bozo
were playing in the forest, it began to rain. They
crept into a hollow tree. Soon the sun shone again,
and suddenly a big, beautiful rainbow came
curving out of the sky and touched the mossy
ground in front of them. Just inside the rainbow
was a pot filled with gold.

"Oh," cried Annie, "What a lovely present
to take to Gran!" She forgot all about Gran's
warning and ran towards the pot. But as
she and Little Dog Bozo went under the
rainbow something very strange happened.
They started to shrink and became smaller and
smaller until they turned into…two little Fairy
Folk! They each now had wings and were
so small that the grass blades were as
tall to them as trees.

"Oh, Bozo!" cried Annie, "How will we find
our way home to Gran to tell her what has
happened to us?" She sat down under a
toadstool and began to cry.

Bozo tried out his wings,
but landed head-over-paws in a clump
of violets. Annie couldn't help laughing.
"We'll have to walk until we learn to fly,"
she said. "Come on, let's go home."

After a while they came to a deep river. "How
shall we get across?" whispered Annie to Bozo.
Just then a frog came out from his moss-covered
house and offered to ferry them across the water.
"What a nice boat!" Annie said as she climbed
in. "It reminds me of something. Why, I do
believe it's one of the boats we made
when we were playing here."
When they reached the other bank Annie
thanked the frog and gave him a
biscuit from her lunch bag.

The sun went down and the forest filled with shadows. Annie and Little Dog Bozo began to feel frightened. Suddenly, a family of mice came scurrying along the path, scaring Bozo. But the mice were friendly and warned the two new Fairy Folk that the big wild cat was out hunting.

"Hurry, he's coming," they said. "Follow us."

So Annie and Little Dog Bozo went home with the mice for supper. They had grasshopper pie and toasted midges, and Annie broke up some biscuits to give to the baby mice. Then they all went to sleep, tucked up small and warm in a soft bed of thistledown. When the moon rose the mice ran out to dance in the moonlight, but Annie and Little Dog Bozo did not wake till sunrise.

The next morning, Annie and Bozo
said goodbye to the mice and set off on their long
walk home. After a while, they rested with some
friendly bluebirds they met on their way.
They ate moth cakes and ant cookies, and
drank tea out of flower cups. Then they all sat on
a wild rose branch and sang some songs until it was
time for them to set off once more on
their journey home.

The next day they met a wise old
Mr. Longlegs who knew almost everything
about everything. After they had told him their
story, he looked at them thoughtfully for a
while, then said:

"I think you had better meet the Fairy King
and Queen and all the other Fairy Folk. Little folk
just like yourselves live in the ferny glade by the
waterfall just down the path."

Annie and Little Dog Bozo felt so
happy to know there were other little people
just like themselves!

They thanked Mr. Longlegs and ran towards
the waterfall which sparkled between the trees.
But suddenly, that wicked wild cat pounced on
Little Dog Bozo and was about
to eat him when…

"Stop that at once," a voice commanded. "Put down that fairy person!" It was the Fairy King. The cat sulkily put down Little Dog Bozo and slunk away. Then the Fairy King led them to the Fairy Court where they met the Fairy Queen.

In the ferny glade were gathered all those who had gone under rainbows at one time or another. The King explained that because Annie and Bozo had not listened to Gran Tibbet's warning they would now be Fairy Folk for ever and ever. They must learn to be good Fairy Folk just like the others. Then all the fairies, elves and pixies came forward to greet them.

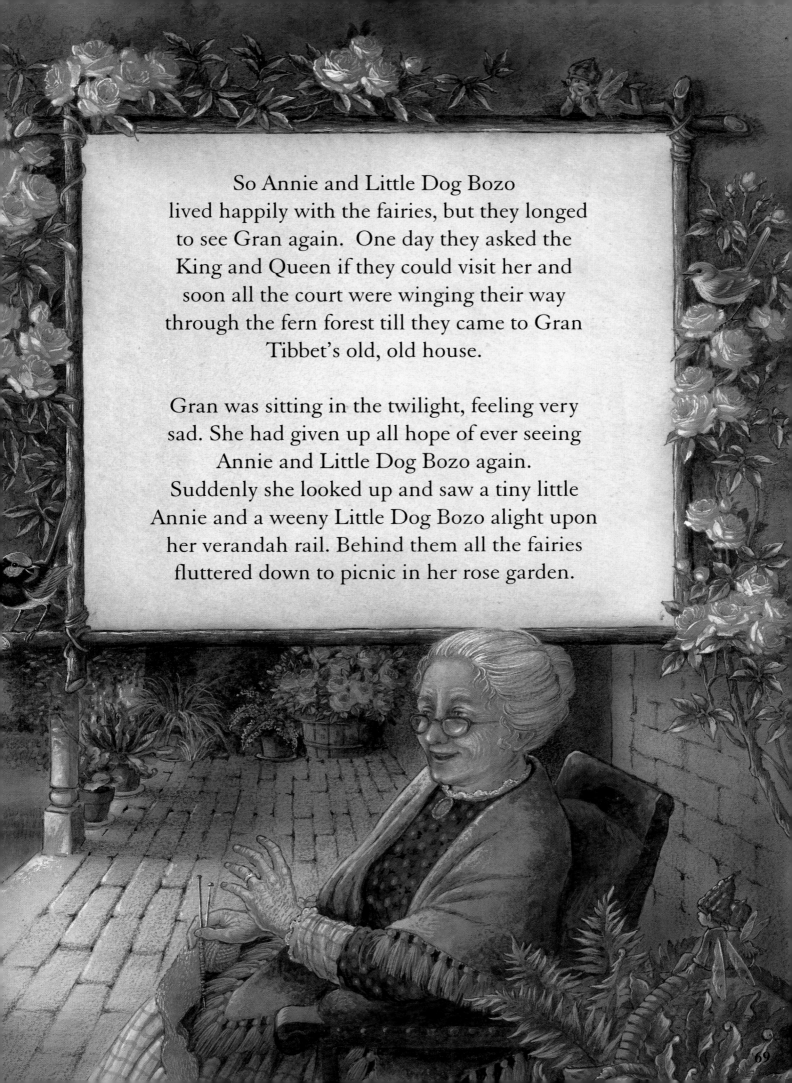

So Annie and Little Dog Bozo
lived happily with the fairies, but they longed
to see Gran again. One day they asked the
King and Queen if they could visit her and
soon all the court were winging their way
through the fern forest till they came to Gran
Tibbet's old, old house.

Gran was sitting in the twilight, feeling very
sad. She had given up all hope of ever seeing
Annie and Little Dog Bozo again.
Suddenly she looked up and saw a tiny little
Annie and a weeny Little Dog Bozo alight upon
her verandah rail. Behind them all the fairies
fluttered down to picnic in her rose garden.

"Look, Gran," cried Annie, "we're safe after all, but we have to be Fairy Folk for ever and ever. We're well and happy, and we've brought a present for you – the pot of gold we found under the rainbow."

So Annie and Little Dog Bozo lived with the Fairy Folk forever, but they often came to talk to Gran while the Fairy Court picnicked in her rose garden. Gran stopped worrying about who would take care of Annie and Little Dog Bozo because she knew that now they could look after themselves.

And what about the pot of gold? Of course it
was only a fairy-sized pot of gold, so Gran set it
on her mantelpiece in a tiny glass case, just to
prove that fairy folk really *did* live in the Fern
Forest and that there really *was* a pot of gold to
be found under the rainbow.

THE TOOTH FAIRY

Tom had a loose tooth. It fell out while he and his sister Holly were playing in the garden.

"Don't lose it," said Holly. "We'll put it in a glass of water. Then tonight we'll wait for the Tooth Fairy to come and collect it."

So Tom put the tooth in his pocket. But when he looked for it at tea-time it had vanished.

After tea, Tom and Holly took a torch and went into the garden to search for the lost tooth, but it was nowhere to be found. Tired and disappointed, they went to bed.

"Now we'll *never* see the Tooth Fairy," sighed Holly, "Last time, when I lost a tooth, I tried so hard to stay awake, but I couldn't. The Tooth Fairy took my tooth, left some money behind, and was gone. I didn't see a thing!"

That night, the children slept soundly. Just as the sun was rising, Tom was woken by a tinkling in the kitchen. He tiptoed in and saw the Tooth Fairy sitting on the window sill.

"Tom," she said softly, "you must search for your missing tooth – it's very important indeed. If you and Holly can find it, I promise to show you my home in the clouds and tell you why I need your tooth."

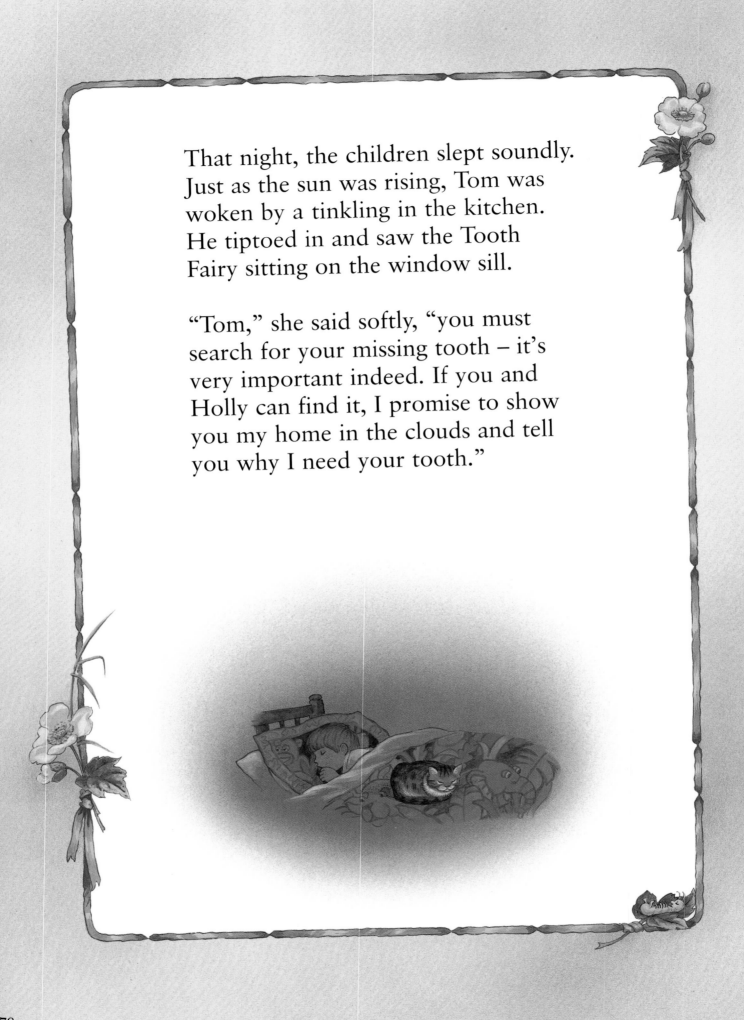

79

So Tom woke up Holly, and together
they ran out into the garden.

Frantically they searched for the
missing tooth. At last, they found it,
shining white amongst the daisies.

"Hooray!" laughed the tooth Fairy.
"Now I'll take you to Cloudland, just
as I promised."

She waved her magic wand, and suddenly
Holly and Tom were as small as the Tooth
Fairy. But before they had time to be
surprised, she waved her wand again and
white doves began to swoop down from
the trees. They had golden bridles and
red velvet saddles.

"Jump on, Holly!" cried Tom. "We're
going for a ride – up into the sky!"

The white doves flew high into the pink dawn sky where amongst the clouds lay a magical land with hills as soft as cotton wool.

They landed beside a beautiful palace surrounded by gardens full of the strangest plants the children had ever seen.

They were silver stars growing like flowers, and tended by pixie gardeners, and moored by a cloud was a boat with rainbow sails.

"Now, Holly and Tom," said the Tooth Fairy, "the stars in the sky eventually grow old and fall down, and the fairies must replace them.

"New stars grow from special star seeds, which are children's baby teeth. That is why when a child's tooth drops out I come down and collect it!"

"But why is my tooth so important?" asked Tom.

"Well," said the Tooth Fairy, "most stars in the sky are silver, but here and there you can see gold ones.

"Now, *your* teeth are very special, Tom, because they will grow into golden stars. And we know an old golden star will fall very soon, and will need to be replaced."

"Look!" cried Holly, "A golden star is falling now!"

"Come, children!" said the Tooth Fairy, taking their hands. "It's time to replace the old golden star. We must hurry and plant Tom's tooth in the sky!"

A silver boat was moored not far from the house. The Tooth Fairy and the children climbed aboard and together they set sail into the sky until they reached the place where the golden star had been.

"Please may I plant my own tooth?" asked Tom.

"Of course," said the Tooth Fairy, and she showed Tom what to do.

The silver boat sailed back to
Cloudland, and the Tooth Fairy and
the children jumped out onto the
clouds. "Soon you must go home,"
said the Tooth Fairy, "but first come
into my house and have some
breakfast."

A bell tinkled and all the pixie
gardeners came scampering inside to
join them. They all had breakfast
together. Then the Tooth Fairy
waved her magic wand and...

Tom found he was back in his bed! Holly came running into his room. "Tom!" she said excitedly. "Did we really see the Tooth Fairy last night? Or was it a dream?"

"It's true!" laughed Tom. "The Tooth Fairy took us with her to Cloudland!" Then they ran to tell their parents.

That night Tom and Holly searched the sky for a glittering new golden star. "Look!" cried Tom, at last. "There it is! That's the one I planted! My very own golden star!"

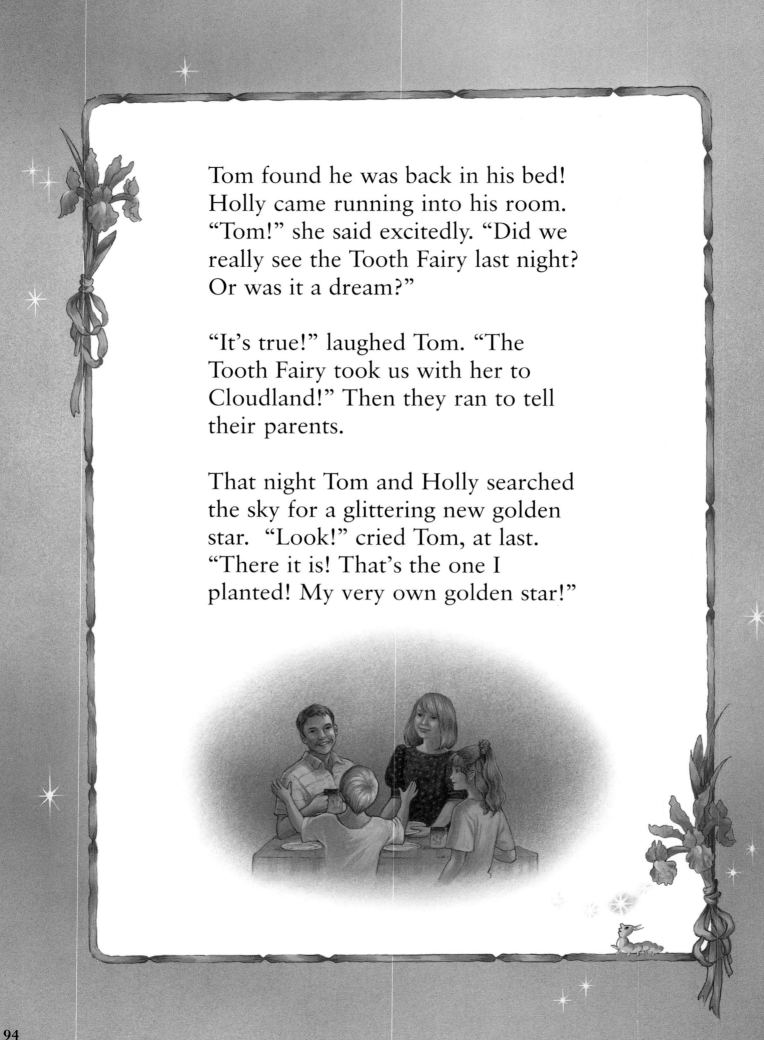

A Visit to FAIRYLAND

Laura said there were fairies at the bottom of the
garden. She said that in the old willow tree there
was a green door and when the fairies opened it
you could see right into Fairyland.

"Yes, dear," said her mother, who was busy
cooking. "Now, why don't you take your little
brother into the garden? You can show him the
fairies and the door to Fairyland."

Laura could tell that her mother thought
she was just pretending and she felt rather
hurt. Still, she took Daniel's hand and
led him into the garden and down towards
the willow tree.

"Ssh, Danny," she whispered. "If we are
very quiet the fairies might open their green
door and come out to talk to us."

Sure enough, after a few minutes the green
door opened... and out came the fairies.

"Would you like to come through this little doorway and see Fairyland?" asked the fairies.

"Oh, yes!" exclaimed Laura excitedly. Then she and Daniel crawled through the doorway and found themselves in Fairyland.

Before them was a toadstool town where pixies and other fairy folk were busy shopping and chatting, just like people. Daniel trotted off chuckling to explore the narrow twisting streets.

"Don't go too far, you might get lost," warned his sister. "Stay close so I can keep an eye on you!"

To Daniel the toadstool houses were just like a
toy village and he wanted to play with the pixies.
Laura watched him running about for a while,
then she noticed further away a garden full of
big flowers.

"Come along, Danny," she coaxed. "Let's go and
look at those beautiful flowers."

The flowers were so large that Daniel soon forgot
the toadstool houses and ran to look at them.
Inside each flower a fairy baby was curled up as if
in its cradle.

"This is where our babies live till they are old
enough to fly," a fairy nurse told the children.

The flower nursery was bathed in warm golden light and soon the children were glad to go into some nearby woods where it was cool and shady. A fern-fringed path led them to a lily pool where fairies were bathing and playing near a crystal spring. Laura and Daniel drank springwater from leaf-cups, and paddled in the shallows. Soon they felt cool enough to explore further.

They followed the path through the woods and before long they heard sweet music: pipes, bells and a tinkling harp. Then, in a clearing edged with flowers, they came upon a group of elfin musicians. Rabbits, mice and frogs all had their parts to play and several fairies were dancing to music.

"There is a ball tonight," the fairies explained to the children, "so we are practising our steps!"

The children wandered on and soon they came to the edge of the woods. There, between twisted tree roots, large caves had formed in a sandy bank. Inside each cave was a kitchen in which elfin cooks were preparing a marvellous feast.

"All these lovely dishes will be served at the ball tonight," the fairies told the children. "The food is cooked here, then taken to the fairy castle in butterfly carriages."

Of course the children felt hungry seeing such lovely food, so the kindly elves invited them to sit down and eat whatever they liked.

While they tried all kinds of dainty and colourful cakes and biscuits, Laura talked to the fairies and elves about life in Fairyland.

"Do you ever have to do any work?" she asked.

"Oh, yes," one silver-haired fairy replied. "My work is to go out and put frost crystals everywhere."

"Why do you do that?" Laura asked, puzzled.

"Well, when the world has been dull and gloomy and you wake to a day where every twig and grass blade sparkles, it's suddenly a beautiful suprise, isnt't it?"

"Oh, yes it is," cried Laura. "Thank you, Silver Fairy, for all your lovely frosty mornings!"

"I too have my work in the world," said an elf, smiling at Laura and Daniel. "With my baskets of toadstools I fly around at first light and I plant bright red ones where I think they will look just right."

"Yes, we've seen them, haven't we, Daniel?" cried Laura excitedly. "You left some spotted ones under the pine trees just outside our garden."

"Now, what would you like to
see next?" the fairies asked the children.

Laura looked at Daniel. "We ought to be going home," she
said regretfully. "our Aunt Kathy is coming to lunch at
our house, and it will be ready soon."

But Daniel wasn't ready to go home, and Laura was afraid
he would make a fuss, so she decided they could stay in
Fairyland for just a little while longer.

"Can we see where you make all your pretty sparkling
dresses?" she asked the fairies.

So the fairies showed the children the little silk spinners
who spend all their time making gossamer-fine
shawls, cloaks and dresses, all delicately
sewn with diamond droplets.

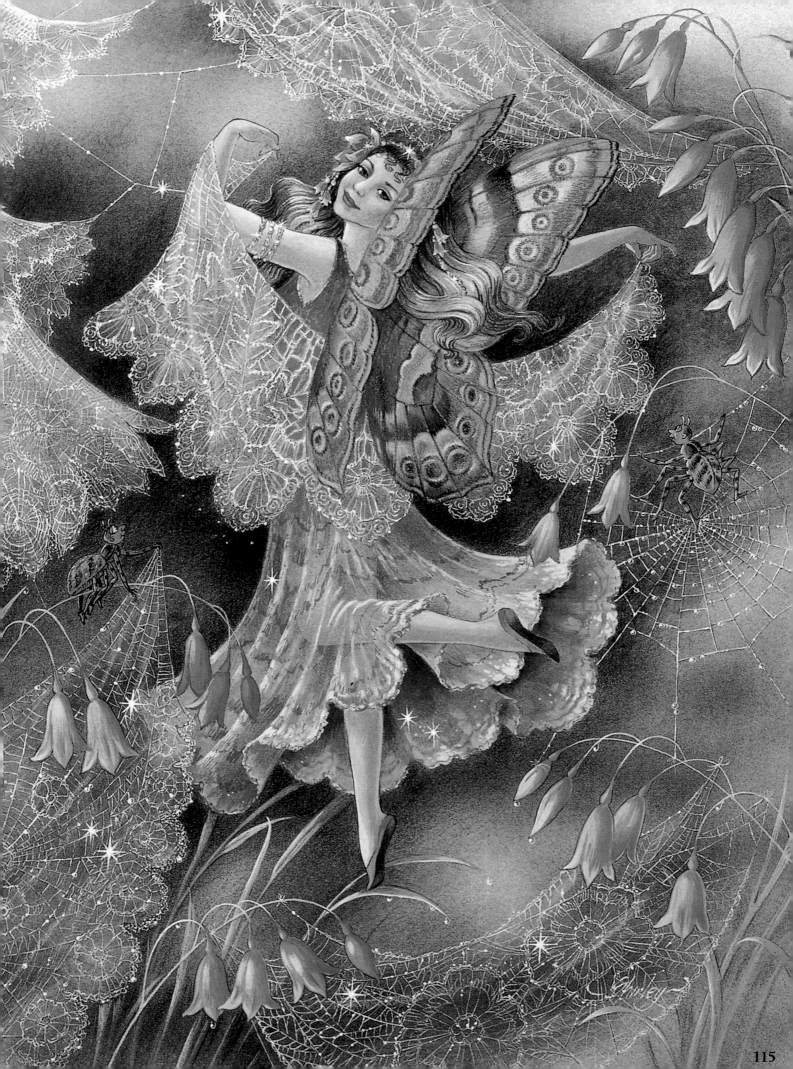

115

"Please show us one last thing before we go home," said Laura. "We'd love to see the fairy castle where you live and where the ball will be held tonight."

So the fairies put Laura and Daniel into a butterfly carriage which floated over the sea to a bay of islands, where a glittering fairy castle stood upon a rocky pinnacle.

While they were circling the castle, Daniel fell asleep in the butterfly carriage. It flew over the forest, the big flowers and the toadstool town before landing at last near the old willow tree.

Laura woke up Daniel, and while he was still too sleepy to protest she helped him crawl back through the little doorway.

"Goodbye, Laura and Daniel," called the fairies. "Be good and kind, and you will see us again soon."

Then the little green door shut and seemed to fade away.

"Come along, Danny," said Laura. "Let's go and have lunch, and we'll tell Mummy all about our visit to Fairyland."

The children found their mother just laying the table for lunch. Their Aunt Kathy had arrived, and she hugged the children and gave each of them a drawing book and a packet of colouring pencils.

"Danny's very good at drawing," Laura told her. "He can draw a box, a ball and a happy face. Danny, draw something for Aunt Kathy."

So Daniel drew a picture. But everyone was very suprised when he didn't draw a box or a ball or a happy face - he drew a fairy instead!

FAIRY BOOK
An Anthology of Verse

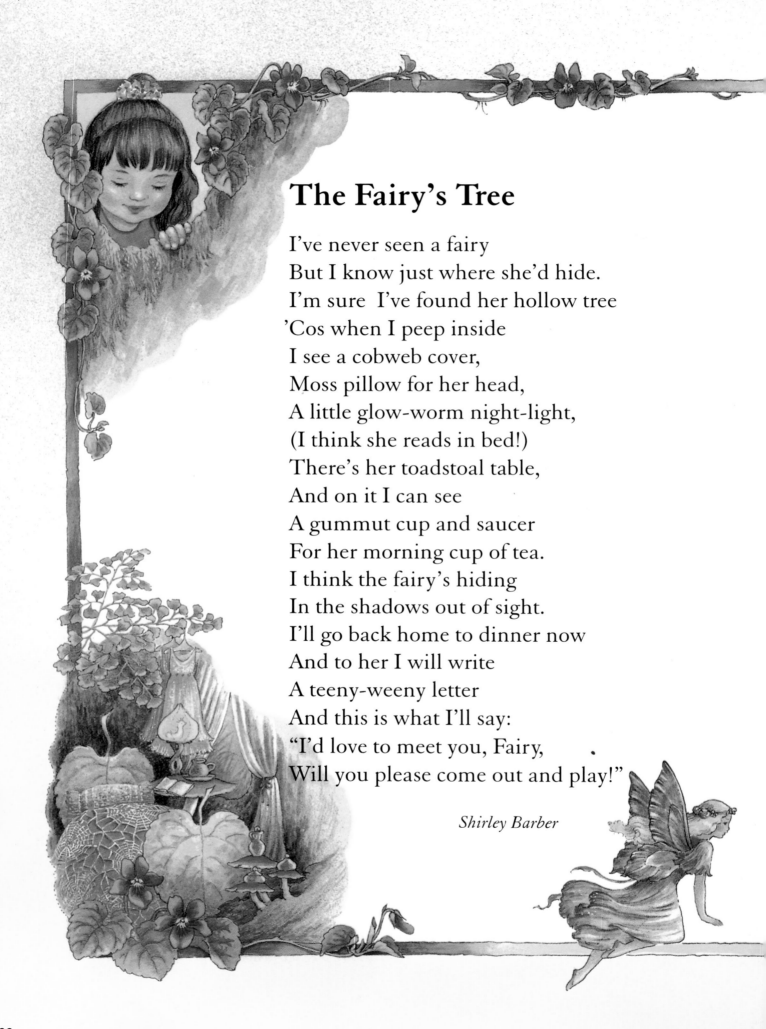

The Fairy's Tree

I've never seen a fairy
But I know just where she'd hide.
I'm sure I've found her hollow tree
'Cos when I peep inside
I see a cobweb cover,
Moss pillow for her head,
A little glow-worm night-light,
(I think she reads in bed!)
There's her toadstool table,
And on it I can see
A gummut cup and saucer
For her morning cup of tea.
I think the fairy's hiding
In the shadows out of sight.
I'll go back home to dinner now
And to her I will write
A teeny-weeny letter
And this is what I'll say:
"I'd love to meet you, Fairy,
Will you please come out and play!"

Shirley Barber

Toadstools

It's not a bit windy,
It's not a bit wet,
The sky is as sunny
As summer, and yet
Little umbrellas are
Everywhere spread,
Pink ones, and brown ones,
And orange, and red.

I can't see the folks
Who are hidden below;
I've peeped, and I've peeped
Round the edges but no!
They hold their umbrellas
So tight and so close
That nothing shows under,
Not even a nose!

Elizabeth Fleming

Bedtime Story

Tell me my favourite story
While I am snuggling down,
About the beautiful fairy
Who wears a sparkling gown.

Tell me about her silken hair,
Her rainbow-coloured wings,
Tell of her bag of magic stars,
Sing me the song she sings.

Tell me she flies through the forest dark
And after a while she hears
A poor little bunny crying,
So, gently she dries his tears.

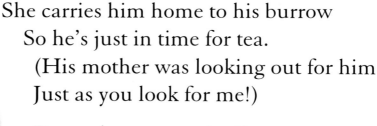

She carries him home to his burrow
So he's just in time for tea.
(His mother was looking out for him
Just as you look for me!)

For an hour or so she lingers.
She sings the bunny to sleep,
Then leaves behind on his pillow
A magical star to keep.

I'll help you remember the wording.
It has to be told just right.
And then you can tell me it
all again
Tomorrow – and every night!

Shirley Barber

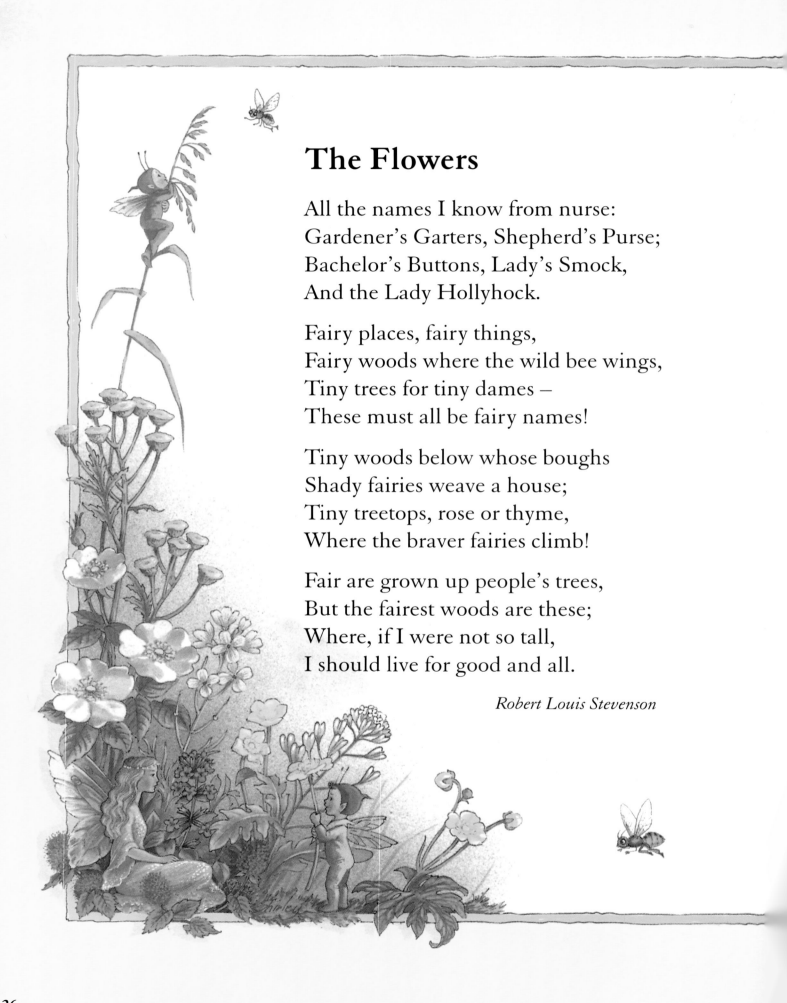

The Flowers

All the names I know from nurse:
Gardener's Garters, Shepherd's Purse;
Bachelor's Buttons, Lady's Smock,
And the Lady Hollyhock.

Fairy places, fairy things,
Fairy woods where the wild bee wings,
Tiny trees for tiny dames –
These must all be fairy names!

Tiny woods below whose boughs
Shady fairies weave a house;
Tiny treetops, rose or thyme,
Where the braver fairies climb!

Fair are grown up people's trees,
But the fairest woods are these;
Where, if I were not so tall,
I should live for good and all.

Robert Louis Stevenson

The Miniature World

If I was very, very small
The jointed grasses would be tall,
And I would climb up them like trees
To wave to passing honey bees.
And then I think I'd like to try
To ride a big blue dragonfly –
Zigzag around the sky like mad
Then land it on a lily-pad.
When I was hungry I would eat
Sorrel, mint and meadow-sweet.
Maybe I'd leapfrog real frogs,
Or maybe dive off mossy logs
Into pools deep, cool and dim,
And with the little tadpoles swim.
Of course, it would be very scary
Meeting spiders, black and hairy!
And those giant drops of dew –
I guess I'd have to dodge them too!
But it would be so nice to know
The hidden paths where Fairies go,
And oh! so good to spend my days
Exploring, secret forest ways...
And when I was too tired to roam
I'd hail a beetle and ride home!

Shirley Barber

The Fairies' Ball

Katie has a fine doll's house,
It stands against the wall;
Her grandma gave it to her and
It's elegant and tall.

Katie said, at midnight,
Or perhaps a little after,
She was woken by the tiny sounds
Of music and of laughter.

She sat up in her bed and thought
She really must be dreaming –
From every little doll's house window
Golden light was streaming.

She crept across to see what could
Be going on in there,
And saw it was a fairies' ball –
A very grand affair.

All night the fairies revelled, then
At dawn, away they flew.
Now Katie's just a little cross
At all there is to do.

She doesn't mind her doll's house used
By fairies and by elves,
But thinks that they should always
Clean up afterwards themselves!

Shirley Barber

The Rainbow Stairway

The lightning made us jump,
The thunder was much too loud,
The rain came down in a torrent,
But now, against the cloud,
The garden glows in the sunlight;
We stare at the golden hill. For look!
Through the sparkling raindrops,
Which gently shower still,
There's a rainbow stairway curving
Down from the sky's grey-blue,
So fairies can climb to their ballroom
Shall we run and climb it too?

Shirley Barber

The Fairy Swing

Down in the apple orchard
White petals fell like rain
Round little Mary Catherine
As she made a daisy-chain.

She used a lot of daisies,
She fashioned it with care –
Heard her mother calling her,
And left it hanging there.

When later she went back again
She heard a wee voice singing,
And in her daisy-chain she saw
A lovely fairy swinging.

Now, Mary Catherine always leaves
Her daisy-chains behind.
If fairies use them for their swings
She says she doesn't mind.

Shirley Barber

Elfin Friends

Uncle William knew an elf,
"A manikin," he said,
"In pointed hat and buckled shoes
And a suit of green and red."

Aunt Betty knew an elf
Of whom she grew quite fond.
They quarelled when he tried to fish
The goldfish from her pond.

My grandma said a little elf
She often used to see.
He'd visit her to chat and drink
A thimbleful of tea.

She knitted him a woolly cap
With flaps to warm his ears,
And he was very grateful –
They were friends for years and years.

They teach you really silly things
When first you go to school,
Like knitting useless woolly snakes
Right through a wooden spool.

But I had such a good idea –
In red and green and white
I've knitted socks for chilly elves,
(I hope they're not too bright!)

If I can stay awake tonight,
And if there is an elf,
And if he likes his socks, I'll have
An elfin friend myself.

Shirley Barber

The Little Elfman

I met a little elfman once,
Down where the lilies blow.
I asked him why he was so small.
And why he didn't grow.

He slightly frowned, and with his eye
He looked me through and through –
"I'm just as big for me," said he,
"As you are big for you!"

John Kendrick Bangs

The Tea Party

A robin brought the message –
She'll come at half-past three.
We'll sit where it is shady
Beneath the willow tree.
I'll make some tiny sandwiches,
Fill flower cups with dew.
A pollen cake I'll try to make
And daisy biscuits too.
I'll lay upon this toadstool
Rose petal plates for three.
The table must look pretty when
A Fairy comes to tea.

Shirley Barber

The Fairy Queen

The woodland is hushed –
It seems to be waiting.
Even the breeze doesn't stir.
Everything seems to be anticipating
A wonderful thing to occur.
Through bluebells and ferns
A green pathway is winding;
Rabbits each side of it sit.
Above them the blossom boughs
Downward are bending
Where small birds excitedly flit.
Hark! there's the sound of a
Small drummer drumming.
Rabbits respectfully stand.
Now, down the pathway
They're coming! They're coming!
A colourful miniature band!
The mice shake the bluebells
And they begin ringing –
The tiniest tinkling sound.
Now come the baby elves
Hopping and springing
Over the soft mossy ground.
And here are the fairies,
(Oh, can I be dreaming?) –
Some flying, some dancing along.
In jewel-bright garments
A-glitter and gleaming,
They sing such a haunting sweet song.
And lastly, the fairest,
Her delicate dress is
Oh, shimmering gold and pale green;
A diamond crown on her
Floating silk tresses –
The beautiful Fairy Queen!

Shirley Barber

135

Fairy Dresses

The other day I woke at dawn,
And tiptoed out onto the lawn,
Then I stared in such surprise
At the sight which met my eyes.
Everywhere I looked there were
Veils of jewelled gossamer.
Where the hollyhocks grow tall
Fairy shawls lay over all;
On the rose-arch, in each space,
Petticoats of finest lace.
On the lupins and the phlox
Hung the daintiest fairy frocks,
Diamond-sprinkled, shimmering,
And, in shadows glimmering,
Sequinned cloaks for evening wear;
Twinkling strands for golden hair.
Someone, (hiding I suppose),
Must have fashioned all those clothes,
Hoped a fairy passing by
Would fly down her dress to buy.
But – whose fingers, small but strong
Had been so busy all night long?

Shirley Barber

Fairy-wear

A Cowslip flower will make a hat
  for any little elf;
With Pennywort umbrellas he
  can always shade himself.
Wild Arum makes both hood and cape
  if it should start to rain,
At night a Lamb's Ear leaf can be
  his furry counterpane.

In the hedge, Convolvulus
  has flowers light and airy;
Neatly pleated flaring dresses
  fit for any fairy.
A spangled wrap of lacy webs
  draped softly over all,
A crown of Hawthorn buds and she
  is ready for the ball.

Shirley Barber

Water Babies

Where do the Water Babies dwell –
Does anyone know, can anyone tell?
"Yes," said a mermaid sweet to me,
"They live beside the bright blue sea.

"Down on the sands they come and play,
They paddle in the sea all day;
With tiny dimpled naked feet,
I've seen them!" cried a mermaid sweet.

And she was right – I've seen them too,
Little white feet in the water blue;
Scampering merrily hand in hand,
All along the golden sand.

No wonder the sea laughs all day long.
And sings them such a happy song;
I've seen them there, so I know well,
That's where the Water Babies dwell.

Unknown

The Mermaid's Child

Down by the sea Louisa found
A mermaid's baby (so she said).
It lay within an ormer shell,
Curled up as if that was its bed.

She fed it sea-foam cake and when
It cried she gave its face a kiss.
She combed its curls, and cuddled it –
Oh! we got very tired of this!

She wouldn't swim or play with us
She stayed beside it all the day.
Thank goodness when the tide came in
The mermaids took their child away.

Shirley Barber

The Dream Fairy

A little fairy comes at night,
Her eyes are blue, her hair is brown,
With silver spots upon her wings,
And from the moon she flutters down.

She has a little silver wand,
And when a good child goes to bed
She waves her wand from right to left
And makes a circle round her head.

And then it dreams of pleasant things,
Of fountains filled with fairy fish,
And trees that bear delicious fruit,
And bow their branches at a wish;

Of arbors filled with dainty scents
From lovely flowers that never fade,
Bright 'flies that flitter in the sun,
And glow-worms shining in the shade;

And talking birds with gifted tongues
For singing songs and telling tales,
And pretty dwarfs to show the way
Through the fairy hills and fairy dales.

Thomas Hood

The Little Folk

In Spring, when the cherry-plum blossom
Lay soft as pink foam in the trees,
I saw them descend on the garden.
At first, sure, I thought it was bees!

Down where the petals were scattered,
Laughing and singing they came.
I watched from my window astonished –
The Little Folk playing a game.

They swung from the flower-laden branches.
They twisted and spun on the wing.
Their singing was sweeter than silver
As they sang and they danced in a ring.

Well! I never saw a sight like it –
The Little Folk all at their play.
Then Pussy ran out from the bushes,
And up they all flew – and away!

Shirley Barber

Midnight Fishing

The crescent moon is riding high
Like a silver ship in the midnight sky.
Those misty veils
Are silken sails
And we can go fishing, you and I.

We'll rock on waves of deepest blue.
We'll cast our nets like the sailors do.
Each shining fish
Is a tiny wish,
And we'll make sure to bring home a few.

We'll moor by a cloud in Scorpio.
You're much braver than I am, so
Lean out and grab
A spangled crab
While I drop my line in the depths below.

We're sailing home by dawn's pink light.
With a glittering crab and the wishes bright,
The silvery gleam
Of a fisherman's dream –
Oh! let's go fishing again tonight.

Shirley Barber

Twelve O'Clock — Fairy-time

Through the house give glimmering light
By the dead and drowsy fire;
Every elf and fairy sprite
Hop as light as bird from brier.

.   .   .

Now, until the break of day,
Through this house each fairy stray.

William Shakespeare

THE MERMAID PRINCESS

In a tropical ocean lay a small green island surrounded by sandy beaches and a coral reef. At high tide, when the sea covered the reef, it flowered like a magical garden - filled with brilliant fish, swaying plants and strange sea creatures. There was only one house on the island in it lived two children, Jon and Wendy, and their parents.

It was holiday time. Jon and Wendy's father spent all day in his boat fishing, and their mother was busy writing a book. Wendy was recovering from the flu, and was too weak to do anything. She just lay on a couch gazing out to sea, or down into the big coral pool not far from her window. Nothing seemed to interest her.

Jon spent his time wandering over the reef at low tide.
When he found something really unusual he would bring it
inside to show Wendy. All the while, he was being
watched by someone very small hidden amongst the coral.
It was Sandy the seashore pixie. Sandy lived in a
sandcastle decorated with bits of green and white
sea-smoothed glass.

149

Early each morning, Sandy pushed his little cart along the tide-line to see what had been washed up. He found bean pods and shells, which he used to keep things in, and sticks for his fire. But what he liked to find most were pieces of coloured glass. He always hoped to find really colourful ones, of sparkling red or blue, but somehow he never did.

One morning, Sandy was amazed to find a beautiful mermaid sitting amidst the coral. She told Sandy that her name was Marina, and that she had been riding on her pet dolphin Silverfin when they were suddenly chased by a huge shark. The dolphin had tossed her ashore, so she would be safe, and then sped off. "But I cut my tail on the sharp coral," she told the pixie, "So now I can't swim home."

Sandy didn't know what to do. He knew that when the tide returned it would sweep the mermaid over the sharp coral and she would be hurt again. Just then Jon appeared on the reef. Sandy quickly hid. To the little pixie, Jon was as big as a giant.

"A real mermaid!" exclaimed Jon. "I've just got to show her to Wendy!" He carefully picked up Marina and carried her back to the coral pool near his sister's window.

Jon ran inside the house. "Wendy!" he called. "I've found a real-live mermaid. I've put her in your coral pool so you can see her through your window."

Wendy sat up and looked out at the pool. Sure enough, there was the mermaid. She was calmly tidying her golden hair. At last something *did* interest Wendy! "Isn't she beautiful!" she cried.

"Yes, but we must keep her a secret," said Jon, "or she might be taken away and put in an aquarium."

That night, when the moon had risen high in the sky, Wendy awoke with a start. She looked out of the window. Yes, the mermaid was still there - and she was talking to a tiny figure! Wendy got up rather shakily and tiptoed to wake Jon. Together they slipped out of the house and down to the coral pool.

At first the mermaid and pixie were too shy to answer Jon and Wendy's eager questions.

"Please talk to us," Wendy begged. "We only want to help you." So Sandy introduced himself and Marina to the children. Then Marina told them her story.

"Somehow we must tell Marina's people where she is so they can come and fetch her," said Jon when she had finished. "I could go," said Sandy. "I have a boat."

Sandy said he would anchor his boat at the edge of the reef and dive down to look for the mermaid's underwater city.

"But how will you breath under water?" asked Jon.

"Seashore pixies can breathe under water as well as on land," Sandy replied.

Marina said he would need a snack for the journey, and gave him some dainty kelp biscuits.

Sandy sailed out over the reef and anchored just beyond it. Then he bravely let himself sink down through the dark water till he landed on the sea-floor. With each surge of the sea he could hear a bell softly chiming. Faint lights glimmered in the distance. Sandy set off over the sand towards them, feeling sure they were coming from the underwater city.

He walked all night. When the sun rose, a soft radiance lit the underwater world, Sandy could now see huge shipwrecks on the sea-floor. Not far from them were open treasure chests which spilled jewels onto the sand. To Sandy the jewels looked like the prettiest bits of coloured glass he had ever seen. He longed to pick some up and take them home, but he didn't because he felt sure they belonged to the mer-people.

At last he could see the underwater city in the distance. He was almost at the end of his journey.

Suddenly shoals of fish swam past him. "Look out, here comes the shark!" they called.

Sandy just had time to hide inside an empty giant clam shell before the shark spotted him.

"You'll have to come out sooner or later," the shark snarled threateningly. Poor Sandy felt very frightened.

Sandy suddenly realised he
was starving. Then he remembered Marina's biscuits,
which he ate straight away. After that he felt a bit
better - but the shark was still circling above.

Suddenly a gleaming white dolphin came flashing
through the water. It was Silverfin. He made straight
for the shark, followed by many other dolphins.
The shark realised he was outnumbered, so
he sped away. Sandy crept out of his
clam shell and gratefully climbed onto
Silverfin's back. Then Silverfin carried
him swiftly to the city of the
mer-people.

Before long, Sandy was telling the mer-people about what had happened to Marina. It turned out that she was a mermaid princess, the youngest daughter of the king. "Take us to her," said the king, so Sandy proudly led the way, on Silverfin, with the mer-king and Marina's sisters and brothers following on their dolphins.

At last they came to Sandy's little boat. He clambered aboard it and carefully steered it between the jagged pieces of coral till he reached the shore. There he found Marina anxiously looking out to sea. He told her that her family was waiting for her beyond the reef.

"But how can I reach them?" she cried. "The coral is so sharp."

Just then, Jon and Wendy came running down. They had seen Sandy returning in his boat. "I'll carry Marina out to where the water is deep enough for her to swim safely," Jon said.

Wendy stood on the beach with Sandy and watched as Jon carried Marina out over the coral. When they had gone beyond the reef Marina said, "Thank you so much. You've all been so kind to me." Then she slipped from Jon's arms. With a splash of her gleaming tail she was on her way.

Marina joyfully greeted her beloved dolphin Silverfin and was soon surrounded by her family and friends. It was a sight that Jon and Wendy would never forget.

Next morning, when Sandy pushed his cart along the tide-line as usual, he was overjoyed to find a thank-you gift from the mer-people.

It was a chest full of brightly coloured jewels! So now Sandy's castle really sparkles in the sunshine - just as he had always dreamed it would.

THE SEVENTH UNICORN

Oak Avenue was a narrow tree-lined street in the oldest part of a large city. Shaded by the oak trees were tall old-fashioned houses, many with high-walled gardens between them where horses and carriages had once been kept.

In more recent times, the ground floors of most of the houses had been turned into quaint-looking shops. Robert and Rachel often came to stay with their Aunt Zelda, who owned a gift shop called The Magic Mirror. The first thing you saw, right at the entrance, was a big mirror in a strangely carved frame. The mirror was so old that the glass was misty and silver-speckled. Rachel felt sure it really *was* a magic mirror.

"If you gaze into it for a long time you begin to see a beautiful world in there, behind the silver speckles," she said. Robert just laughed, but Aunt Zelda said, "You might see it more clearly if you gave the mirror a good polish."

So early next morning, before anyone was about, the children polished the mirror. Robert was impatient to go to the park at the end of the street to try out a new giant slide. As soon as they'd finished cleaning the mirror he ran off. Rachel was about to join him when a sudden movement made her glance back at the mirror.

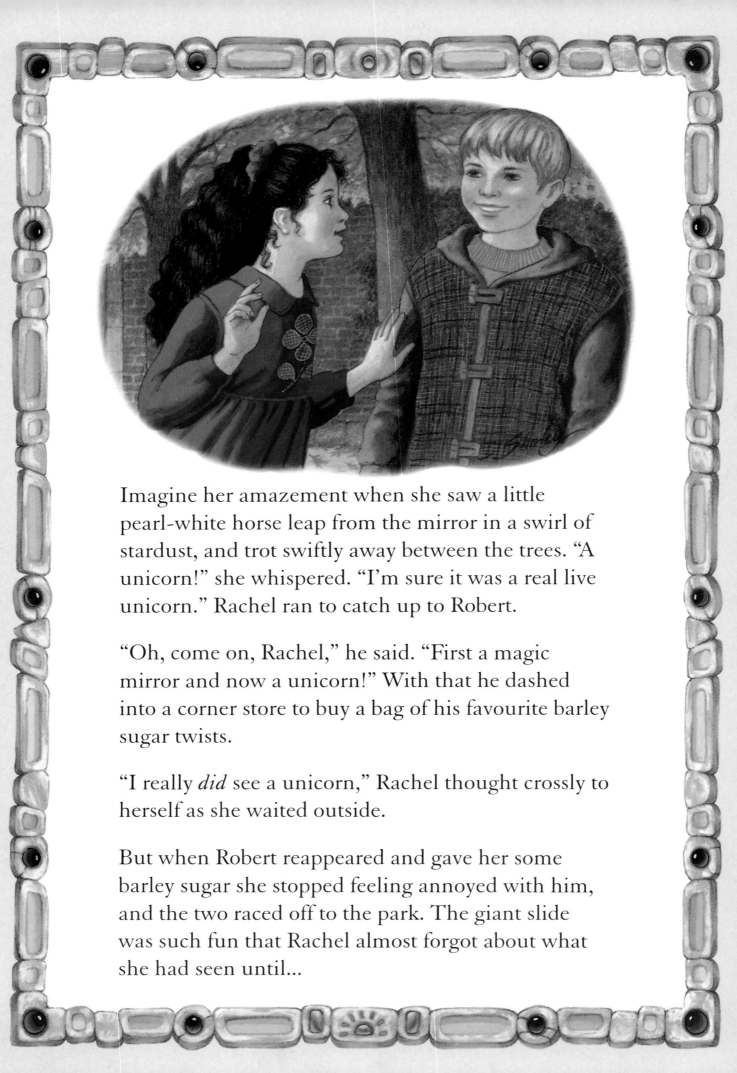

Imagine her amazement when she saw a little pearl-white horse leap from the mirror in a swirl of stardust, and trot swiftly away between the trees. "A unicorn!" she whispered. "I'm sure it was a real live unicorn." Rachel ran to catch up to Robert.

"Oh, come on, Rachel," he said. "First a magic mirror and now a unicorn!" With that he dashed into a corner store to buy a bag of his favourite barley sugar twists.

"I really *did* see a unicorn," Rachel thought crossly to herself as she waited outside.

But when Robert reappeared and gave her some barley sugar she stopped feeling annoyed with him, and the two raced off to the park. The giant slide was such fun that Rachel almost forgot about what she had seen until...

...the little white unicorn trotted into view! His horn and hooves were golden and stardust glittered in his mane and tail. He came right up to the children, as if he wanted to play. "What did I tell you?" Rachel whispered. "Isn't he beautiful!" "Yes! And he absolutely loves barley sugar!" laughed Robert.

The honking of a distant car-horn startled the
unicorn and he suddenly wheeled in a cloud of
stardust and galloped away, his golden hooves silent
on the autumn leaves.

"Let's go back and tell Aunt Zelda that her mirror
really *is* magic!" said Rachel. So the children
hurried back along Oak Avenue, but this time on the
other side. As they were passing the high-walled
yard next to The Wizard's Castle, an antique shop,
Robert stopped suddenly.

"What is it?" asked Rachel. Without replying,
Robert scrambledup the nearest oak tree and peered
over the wall. "Rachel," he called down softly.
"There are six more unicorns in there. They're all
tied up, and they look very unhappy."

"Come down quickly!" hissed Rachel. "Someone's coming!" Down slid Robert, just in time.

A man had unlocked the shop door and was carrying out a strange assortment of antiques to arrange on the pavement outside. He wore a wizard's pointed hat with the name of his shop on it, and a cloak sewn with stars, so that he looked just like a real wizard. When he went back into the shop the children sped past and up the avenue towards Aunt Zelda's gift shop.

The children were almost at Aunt Zelda's shop when the seventh unicorn cantered past. Right before their eyes, he leapt back into the mirror.

"Come on!" cried Robert. "Follow him!" Despite his sister's protest, Robert pulled her with him into the mirror, and they went through the glass as if it were water.

On the other side of the
mirror Rachel's nervousness
faded as she saw they
had entered a beautiful
land, strangely shadowed
at the edges but filled
with jewelled flowers
and grasses.

"Welcome to Arcadia," said a soft voice behind them. Rachel and Robert turned and saw a group of beautiful children. "Or welcome to what is left of Arcadia," said their leader. "For see how on every side a shadow creeps to destroy our lovely world."

Rachel and Robert looked where the girl pointed. They realised that what they had thought was a shadow was a really a creeping fog which had withered flowers and trees where it touched them.

"An evil wizard discovered the spell to open a door into our world," continued the young Arcadian leader. "Each day he entered thourgh the magic mirror, bound a unicorn with a magic halter and led it away. When he steals our last unicorn, Arcadia will be destroyed - only the power of seven unicorns keeps our world whole and well. We sent our seventh unicorn through the mirror to seek out the other six, but he couldn't find them."

Rachel and Robert looked at each other. *They* knew where the missing unicorns were. The wizard must have entered the magic mirror while Aunt Zelda was at the back of the shop.

The children quickly jumped through the magic mirror into the shop. Excitedly they told their amazed aunt all that had happened.

"We must work out a plan to rescue the other unicorns," she said, once she had recovered from her suprise. "We'll have to start very early in the morning before the wizard is out of bed - and we'll need a big bag of barley sugar!"

Next morning at sunrise, while Aunt Zelda guarded the magic mirror doorway, Rachel and Robert ran down Oak Avenue. Rachel kept a lookout for the wizard while Robert climbed over the wall to where the unicorns huddled miserably together.

He quietly unbolted the big gate and pulled off the magic halters, one by one. The six unicorns silently trotted out into the street, where Rachel gave them each some barley sugar. Soon the two children were running full speed up the avenue with the hungry unicorns following close behind.

Aunt Zelda was anxiously waiting outside her gift shop, ready to guide the unicorns back to Arcadia. Rachel leapt through the mirror, ahead of the unicorns, and threw handfuls of barley sugar among the jewelled flowers. The six unicorns followed her back into their own world, and began to crunch the barley sugar.

Next came Robert and Aunt Zelda. With cries of joy the Arcadians came running to hug and pet their unicorns, all seven together again at last. Then, golden light filled the land and the dark shadows were driven away.

For a moment they stood watching,
then Aunt Zelda drew the children
back to their own world...

... only to come face to face with the furious wizard!

"Let me pass!" he thundered. "I need the power of the unicorns to be the greatest wizard in the world."

Aunt Zelda quickly snatched up a heavy candlestick and shattered the mirror!

"The door is closed now," she said. "Arcadia is safe from you forever!"

The wizard scowled horribly, then stamped back to his antique shop and slammed the door.

Aunt Zelda and the children were overjoyed that they had saved Arcadia from the wizard. They knew they would never forget that beautiful world as long as they lived. The ornate mirror frame was soon fitted with a new glass, and although it was no longer a doorway into another world, Rachel and Robert often gazed into it. Sometimes they could just make out a shimmering pearly form. They were sure it was a unicorn looking out at them - perhaps he was thinking about barley sugar!